A Plea For Old Cap Collier

Irvin S. Cobb

Contents

A PLEA FOR OLD
CAP COLLIER

BY

Irvin S. Cobb

A Plea for Old Cap Collier

For a good many years now I have been carrying this idea round with me. It was more or less of a loose and unformed idea, and it wouldn't jell. What brought it round to the solidification point was this: Here the other week, being half sick, I was laid up over Sunday in a small hotel in a small seacoast town. I had read all the newspapers and all the magazines I could get hold of. The local bookstore, of course, was closed. They won't let the oysters stay open on Sunday in that town. The only literature my fellow guests seemed interested in was mail-order tabs and price currents.

Finally, when despair was about to claim me for her own, I ran across an ancient Fifth Reader, all tattered and stained and having that smell of age which is common to old books and old sheep. I took it up to bed with me, and I read it through from cover to cover. Long before I was through the very idea which for so long had been sloshing round inside of my head—this idea which, as one might say, had been aged in the wood—took shape. Then and there I decided that the very first chance I had I would sit me down and write a plea for Old Cap Collier.

In my youth I was spanked freely and frequently for doing many different things that were forbidden, and also for doing the same thing many different times and getting caught doing it. That, of course, was before the Boy Scout movement had come along to show how easily and how sanely a boy's natural restlessness and a boy's natural love for adventure may be directed into helpful channels; that was when nearly everything a normal, active boy craved to do was wrong and, therefore, held to be a spankable offense.

This was a general rule in our town. It did not especially apply to any particular household, but it applied practically to all the households with which I was in any way familiar. It was a community where an old-fashioned brand of applied theology was most strictly applied. Heaven was a place which went unanimously Democratic every fall, because all the Republicans had gone elsewhere. Hell was a place full of red-hot coals and clinkered sinners and un-baptized babies and a smell like somebody cooking ham, with a deputy devil coming in of a morning with an asbestos napkin draped over his arm and flicking a fireproof cockroach off the table cloth and leaning across the back of Satan's chair and saying: "Good mornin', boss. How're you going to have your lost souls this mornin'—fried on one side or turned over?"

Sunday was three weeks long, and longer than that if it rained. About all a fellow could do after he'd come back from Sunday school was to sit round with his feet cramped into the shoes and stockings which he never wore on week days and with the rest of him incased in starchy, uncomfortable dress-up clothes—just sit round and sit round and itch. You couldn't scratch hard either. It was sinful to scratch audibly and with good, broad, free strokes, which is the only satisfactory way to scratch. In our town they didn't spend Sunday; they kept the Sabbath, which is a very different thing.

Looking back on my juvenile years it seems to me that, generally speaking, when spanked I deserved it. But always there were two punishable things against which— being disciplined—my youthful spirit revolted with a sort of inarticulate sense of injustice. One was for violation of the Sunday code, which struck me as wrong—the code, I mean, not the violation—without knowing exactly why it was wrong; and the other, repeated times without number, was when I had been caught reading nickul libruries, erroneously referred to by our elders as dime novels.

I read them at every chance; so did every normal boy of my acquaintance. We traded lesser treasures for them; we swapped them on the basis of two old volumes for one new one; we maintained a clandestine circulating-library system which had its branch offices in every stable loft in our part of town. The more daring among us read them in school behind the shelter of an open geography propped up on the desk.

Shall you ever forget the horror of the moment when, carried away on the wings of adventure with Nick Carter or Big-Foot Wallace or Frank Reade or bully Old Cap, you forgot to flash occasional glances of cautious inquiry forward in order to make sure the teacher was where she properly should be, at her desk up in front, and read on and on until that subtle sixth sense which comes to you when a lot of people begin staring at you warned you something was amiss, and you looked up and round you and found yourself all surrounded by a ring of cruel, gloating eyes?

I say cruel advisedly, because up to a certain age children are naturally more cruel than tigers. Civilization has provided them with tools, as it were, for practicing cruelty, whereas the tiger must rely only on his teeth and his bare claws. So you looked round, feeling that the shadow of an impending doom encompassed you, and then you realized that for no telling how long the teacher had been standing just behind you, reading over your shoulder.

And at home were you caught in the act of reading them, or—what from the parental standpoint was almost as bad—in the act of harboring them? I was. Housecleaning times, when they found them hidden under furniture or tucked away on the back shelves of pantry closets, I was paddled until I had the feelings of a slice of hot, buttered toast somewhat scorched on the under side. And each time, having been paddled, I was admonished that boys who read dime novels—only they weren't dime novels at all but cost uniformly five cents a copy—always came to a bad end, growing up to be criminals or Republicans or something equally abhorrent. And I was urged to read books which would help me to shape my career in a proper course. Such books were put into my hands, and I loathed them. I know now why when I grew up my gorge rose and my appetite turned against so-called classics. Their style was so much like the style of the books which older people wanted me to read when I was in my early teens.

Such were the specious statements advanced by the oldsters. And we had no reply for their argument, or if we had one could not find the language in which to couch it. Besides there was another and a deeper reason. A boy, being what he is, the most sensitive and the most secretive of living creatures regarding his innermost emotions, rarely does bare his real thoughts to his elders, for they, alas, are not young enough to have a fellow feeling, and they are too old and they know too much to be really wise.

What we might have answered, had we had the verbal facility and had we not feared further painful corporeal measures for talking back—or what was worse, ridicule— was that reading Old Cap Collier never yet sent a boy to a bad end. I never heard of a boy who ran away from home and really made a go of it who was actuated at the start by the nickul librury. Burning with a sense of injustice, filled up with the realization that we were not appreciated at home, we often talked of running away and going out West to fight Indians, but we never did. I remember once two of us started for the Far West, and got nearly as far as Oak Grove Cemetery, when—the dusk of evening impending—we decided to turn back and give our parents just one more chance to understand us.

What, also, we might have pointed out was that in a five-cent story the villain was absolutely sure of receiving suitable and adequate punishment for his misdeeds.

Right then and there, on the spot, he got his. And the heroine was always so pluperfectly pure. And the hero always was a hero to his finger tips, never doing anything unmanly or wrong or cowardly, and always using the most respectful language in the presence of the opposite sex. There was never any sex problem in a nickùl librury. There were never any smutty words or questionable phrases. If a villain said "Curse you!" he was going pretty far. Any one of us might whet up our natural instincts for cruelty on Foxe's Book of Martyrs, or read of all manner of unmentionable horrors in the Old Testament, but except surreptitiously we couldn't walk with Nick Carter, whose motives were ever pure and who never used the naughty word even in the passion of the death grapple with the top-booted forces of sinister evil

We might have told our parents, had we had the words in which to state the case and they but the patience to listen, that in a nickul librury there was logic and the thrill of swift action and the sharp spice of adventure. There, invariably virtue was rewarded and villainy confounded; there, inevitably was the final triumph for law and for justice and for the right; there embalmed in one thin paper volume, was all that Sandford and Merton lacked; all that the Rollo books never had. We might have told them that though the Leather-stocking Tales and Robinson Crusoe and Two Years Before the Mast and Ivanhoe were all well enough in their way, the trouble with them was that they mainly were so long-winded. It took so much time to get to where the first punch was, whereas Ned Buntline or Col. Prentiss Ingraham would hand you an exciting jolt on the very first page, and sometimes in the very first paragraph.

You take J. Fenimore Cooper now. He meant well and he had ideas, but his Indians were so everlastingly slow about getting under way with their scalping operations! Chapter after chapter there was so much fashionable and difficult language that the plot was smothered. You couldn't see the woods for the trees.

But it was the accidental finding of an ancient and reminiscent volume one Sunday in a little hotel which gave me the cue to what really made us such confirmed rebels against constituted authority, in a literary way of speaking. The thing which inspired us with hatred for the so-called juvenile classic was a thing which struck deeper even than the sentiments I have been trying to describe.

The basic reason, the underlying motive, lay in the fact that in the schoolbooks of our adolescence, and notably in the school readers, our young mentalities were fed forcibly on a pap which affronted our intelligence at the same time that it cloyed our adolescent palates. It was not altogether the lack of action; it was more the lack of plain common sense in the literary spoon victuals which they ladled into us at school that caused our youthful souls to revolt. In the final analysis it was this more than any other cause which sent us up to the haymow for delicious, forbidden hours in the company of Calamity Jane and Wild Bill Hickok.

Midway of the old dog-eared reader which I picked up that day I came across a typical example of the sort of stuff I mean. I hadn't seen it before in twenty-five years; but now, seeing it, I remembered it as clearly almost as though it had been the week before instead of a quarter of a century before when for the first time it had been brought to my attention. It was a piece entitled, The Shipwreck, and it began as follows:

In the winter of 1824 Lieutenant G—, of the United States Navy, with his beautiful wife and child, embarked in a packet at Norfolk bound to South Carolina.

So far so good. At least, here is a direct beginning. A family group is going somewhere. There is an implied promise that before they have traveled very far something of interest to the reader will happen to them. Sure enough, the packet runs into a storm and founders. As she is going down Lieutenant G—puts his wife and baby into a lifeboat manned by sailors, and then—there being no room for him in the lifeboat—lie remains behind upon the deck of the sinking vessel, while the lifeboat puts off for shore. A giant wave overturns the burdened cockleshell and he sees its passengers engulfed in the waters. Up to this point the chronicle has been what a chronicle should be. Perhaps the phraseology has been a trifle toploftical, and there are a few words in it long enough to run as serials, yet at any rate we are getting an effect in drama. But bear with me while I quote the next paragraph, just as I copied it down:

The wretched husband saw but too distinctly the destruction of all he held dear. But here alas and forever were shut off from him all sublunary prospects. He fell upon the deck—powerless, senseless, a corpse—the victim of a sublime sensibility!

There's language for you! How different it is from that historic passage when the crack of Little Sure Shot's rifle rang out and another Redskin bit the dust. Nothing is said there about anybody having his sublunary prospects shut off; nothing about the Redskin becoming the victim of a sublime sensibility. In fifteen graphic words and in one sentence Little Sure Shot croaked him, and then with bated breath you moved on to the next paragraph, sure of finding in it yet more attractive casualties snappily narrated.

No, sir! In the nickul librury the author did not waste his time and yours telling you that an individual on becoming a corpse would simultaneously become powerless and senseless. He credited your intelligence for something. For contrast, take the immortal work entitled Deadwood Dick of Deadwood; or, The Picked Party; by Edward L. Wheeler, a copy of which has just come to my attention again nearly thirty years after the time of my first reading of it. Consider the opening paragraph:

The sun was just kissing the mountain tops that frowned down upon Billy-Goat Gulch, and in the aforesaid mighty seam in the face of mighty Nature the shadows of a warm June night were gathering rapidly.

The birds had mostly hushed their songs and flown to their nests in the dismal lonely pines, and only the tuneful twang of a well-played banjo aroused the brooding quiet, save it be the shrill, croaking screams of a crow, perched upon the top of a dead pine, which rose from the nearly perpendicular mountain side that retreated in the ascending from the gulch bottom.

That, as I recall, was a powerfully long bit of description for a nickul librury, and having got it out of his system Mr. Wheeler wasted no more valuable space on the scenery. From this point on he gave you action—action with reason behind it and logic to it and the guaranty of a proper climax and a satisfactory conclusion to follow. Deadwood Dick marched many a flower-strewn mile through my young life, but to the best of my recollection he never shut off anybody's sublunary prospects. If a party deserved killing Deadwood just naturally up and killed him, and the historian told about it in graphic yet straightforward terms of speech; and that was all there was to it, and that was all there should have been to it.

At the risk of being termed an iconoclast and a smasher of the pure high ideals of the olden days, I propose to undertake to show that practically all of the preposterous asses and the impossible idiots of literature found their way into the school readers of my generation. With the passage of years there may have been some reform in this direction, but I dare affirm, without having positive knowledge of the facts, that a majority of these half-wits still are being featured in the grammar-grade literature of the present time. The authors of school readers, even modern school readers, surely are no smarter than the run of grown-ups even, say, as you and as I; and we blindly go on holding up as examples before the eyes of the young of the period the characters and the acts of certain popular figures of poetry and prose who—did but we give them the acid test of reason—would reveal themselves either as incurable idiots, or else as figures in scenes and incidents which physically could never have occurred.

You remember, don't you, the school-book classic of the noble lad who by reason of his neat dress, and by his use in the most casual conversation of the sort of language which the late Mr. Henry James used when he was writing his very Jamesiest, se-cured a job as a trusted messenger in the large city store or in the city's large store, if we are going to be purists about it, as the boy in question undoubtedly was?

It seems that he had supported his widowed mother and a large family of brothers and sisters by shoveling snow and, I think, laying brick or something of that techni-cal nature; After this lapse of years I won't be sure about the bricklaying, but at any rate, work was slack in his regular line, and so he went to the proprietor of this vast retail establishment and procured a responsible position on the strength of his easy and graceful personal address and his employment of some of the most stylish ad-jectives in the dictionary. At this time he was nearly seven years old—yes, sir, actu-ally nearly seven. We have the word of the schoolbook for it. We should have had a second chapter on this boy. Probably at nine he was being considered for president of Yale—no, Harvard. He would know too much to be president of Yale.

Then there was the familiar instance of the Spartan youth who having stolen a fox and hidden it inside his robe calmly stood up and let the animal gnaw his vitals rath-er than be caught with it in his possession. But, why? I ask you, why? What was the good of it all? What object was served? To begin with, the boy had absconded with somebody else's fox, or with somebody's else fox, which is undoubtedly the way a compiler of school readers would phrase it. This, right at the beginning, makes the morality of the transaction highly dubious. In the second place, he showed poor taste. If he was going to swipe something, why should he not have swiped a chicken or something else of practical value?

We waive that point, though, and come to the lack of discretion shown by the fox. He starts eating his way out through the boy, a mussy and difficult procedure, when merely by biting an aperture in the tunic he could have emerged by the front way with ease and dispatch. And what is the final upshot of it all? The boy falls dead, with a large unsightly gap in the middle of him. Probably, too, he was a boy whose parents were raising him for their own purposes. As it is, all gnawed up in this fashion and deceased besides, he loses his attractions for everyone except the undertaker. The fox presumably has an attack of acute indigestion. And there you are! Compare the moral of this with the moral of any one of the Old Cap Collier series, where virtue comes into its own and sanity is prevalent throughout and vice gets what it deserves, and all.

In McGuffey's Third Reader, I think it was, occurred that story about the small boy who lived in Holland among the dikes and dams, and one evening he went across the country to carry a few illustrated post cards or some equally suitable gift to a poor blind man, and on his way back home in the twilight he discovered a leak in the sea wall. If he went for help the breach might widen while he was gone and the whole structure give way, and then the sea would come roaring in, carrying death and destruction and windmills and wooden shoes and pineapple cheeses on its crest. At least, this is the inference one gathers from reading Mr. McGuffey's account of the affair.

So what does the quick-witted youngster do? He shoves his little arm in the crevice on the inner side, where already the water is trickling through, thus blocking the leak. All night long he stays there, one small, half-frozen Dutch boy holding back the entire North Atlantic. Not until centuries later, when Judge Alton B. Parker runs for president against Colonel Roosevelt and is defeated practically by acclamation, is there to be presented so historic and so magnificent an example of a contest against tremendous odds. In the morning a peasant, going out to mow the tulip beds, finds the little fellow crouched at the foot of the dike and inquires what ails him. The lad, raising his weary head—but wait, I shall quote the exact language of the book:

"I am hindering the sea from running in," was the simply reply of the child.

Simple? I'll say it is! Positively nothing could be simpler unless it be the stark simplicity of the mind of an author who figures that when the Atlantic Ocean starts boring its way through a crack in a sea wall you can stop it by plugging the hole on the inner side of the sea wall with a small boy's arm. Ned Buntline may never have enjoyed the vogue among parents and teachers that Mr. McGuffey enjoyed, but I'll say this for him—he knew more about the laws of hydraulics than McGuffey ever dreamed.

And there was Peter Hurdle, the ragged lad who engaged in a long but tiresome conversation with the philanthropic and inquisitive Mr. Lenox, during the course of which it developed that Peter didn't want anything. When it came on to storm he got under a tree. When he was hungry he ate a raw turnip. Raw turnips, it would appear, grew all the year round in the fields of the favored land where Peter resided. If the chill winds of autumn blew in through one of the holes in Peter's trousers they blew right out again through another hole. And he didn't care to accept the dime which Mr. Lenox in an excess of generosity offered him, because, it seemed, he already had a dime. When it came to being plumb contented there probably never was a soul on this earth that was the equal of Master Hurdle. He even was satisfied with his name, which I would regard as the ultimate test.

Likewise, there was the case of Hugh Idle and Mr. Toil. Perhaps you recall that moving story? Hugh tries to dodge work; wherever he goes he finds Mr. Toil in one guise or another but always with the same harsh voice and the same frowning eyes, bossing some job in a manner which would cost him his boss-ship right off the reel in these times when union labor is so touchy. And what is the moral to be drawn from this narrative? I know that all my life I have been trying to get away from work, feeling that I was intended for leisure, though never finding time somehow to take it up seriously. But what was the use of trying to discourage me from this agreeable idea back yonder in the formulative period of my earlier years?

In Harper's Fourth Reader, edition of 1888, I found an article entitled The Difference Between the Plants and Animals. It takes up several pages and includes some of the fanciest language the senior Mr. Harper could disinter from the unabridged. In my own case—and I think I was no more observant than the average urchin of my age—I can scarcely remember a time when I could not readily determine certain basic distinctions between such plants and such animals as a child, is likely to encounter in the temperate parts of North America,

While emerging from infancy some of my contemporaries may have fallen into the error of the little boy who came into the house with a haunted look in his eye and asked his mother if mulberries had six legs apiece and ran round in the dust of the road, and when she told him that such was not the case with mulberries he said: "Then, mother, I feel that I have made a mistake."

To the best of my recollection, I never made this mistake, or at least if I did I am sure I made no inquiry afterward which might tend further to increase my doubts; and in any event I am sure that by the time I was old enough to stumble over Mr. Harper's favorite big words I was old enough to tell the difference between an ordinary animal—say, a house cat—and any one of the commoner forms of plant life, such as, for example, the scaly-bark hickory tree, practically at a glance. I'll add this too: Nick Carter never wasted any of the golden moments which he and I spent together in elucidating for me the radical points of difference between the plants and the animals.

In the range of poetry selected by the compilers of the readers for my especial benefit as I progressed onward from the primary class into the grammar grades I find on examination of these earlier American authorities an even greater array of chuckleheads than appear in the prose divisions. I shall pass over the celebrated instance—as read by us in class in a loud tone of voice and without halt for inflection or the taking of breath—of the Turk who at midnight in his guarded tent was dreaming of the hour when Greece her knees in suppliance bent would tremble at his power. I remember how vaguely I used to wonder who it was that was going to grease her knees and why she should feel called upon to have them greased at all. Also, I shall pass over the instance of

Abou Ben Adhem, whose name led all the rest in the golden book in which the angel was writing. Why shouldn't it have led all the rest? A man whose front name begins with Ab, whose middle initial is B, and whose last name begins with Ad will be found leading all the rest in any city directory or any telephone list anywhere. Alphabetically organized as he was, Mr. Adhem just naturally had to lead; and yet for hours on end my teacher consumed her energies and mine in a more or less unsuccessful effort to cause me to memorize the details as set forth by Mr. Leigh Hunt.

In three separate schoolbooks, each the work of a different compilator, I discover Sir Walter Scott's poetic contribution touching on Young Lochinvar—Young Lochinvar who came out of the West, the same as the Plumb plan subsequently came, and the Hiram Johnson presidential boom and the initiative and the referendum and the I. W. W. Even in those ancient times the West appears to have been a favorite place for upsetting things to come from; so I can't take issue with Sir Walter there. But I do take issue with him where he says:

So light to the croupe the fair lady he swung,
So light to the saddle before her he sprung!

Even in childhood's hour I am sure I must have questioned the ability of Young Lochinvar to perform this achievement, for I was born and brought up in a horseback-riding country. Now in the light of yet fuller experience I wish Sir Walter were alive to-day so I might argue the question out with him.

Let us consider the statement on its physical merits solely. Here we have Young Lochinvar swinging the lady to the croupe, and then he springs to the saddle in front of her. Now to do this he must either take a long running start and leapfrog clear over the lady's head as she sits there, and land accurately in the saddle, which is scarcely a proper thing to do to any lady, aside from the difficulty of springing ten or fifteen feet into the air and coming down, crotched out, on a given spot, or else he must contribute a feat in contortion the like of which has never been duplicated since.

To be brutally frank about it, the thing just naturally is not possible. I don't care if Young Lochinvar was as limber as a yard of fresh tripe—and he certainly did shake a lithesome calf in the measures of the dance if Sir Walter, in an earlier stanza, is to be credited with veracity. Even so, I deny that he could have done that croupe trick. There isn't a croupier at Monte Carlo who could have done it. Buffalo Bill couldn't have done it. Ned Buntline wouldn't have had Buffalo Bill trying to do it. Doug Fairbanks couldn't do it. I couldn't do it myself.

Skipping over Robert Southey's tiresome redundancy in spending so much of his time and mine, when I was in the Fifth-Reader stage, in telling how the waters came down at Ladore when it was a petrified cinch that they, being waters, would have to come down, anyhow, I would next direct your attention to two of the foremost idiots in all the realm of poesy; one a young idiot and one an older idiot, probably with whiskers, but both embalmed in verse, and both, mind you, stuck into every orthodox reader to be glorified before the eyes of childhood. I refer to that juvenile champion among idiots, the boy who stood on the burning deck, and to the ship's captain in the poem called The Tempest. Let us briefly consider the given facts as regards the latter: It was winter and it was midnight and a storm was on the deep, and the passengers were huddled in the cabin and not a soul would dare to sleep, and they were shuddering there in silence—one gathers the silence was so deep you could hear them shuddering—and the stoutest held his breath, which is considerable feat, as I can testify, because the stouter a fellow gets the harder it is for him to hold his breath for any considerable period of time. Very well, then, this is the condition of affairs. If ever there was a time when those in authority should avoid spreading alarm this was the time. By all the traditions of the maritime service it devolved upon the skipper to remain calm, cool and collected. But what does the poet reveal to a lot of trusting school children?

"We are lost !" the captain shouted,
As he staggered down the stair.

He didn't whisper it; he didn't tell it to a friend in confidence; he bellowed it out at the top of his voice so all the passengers could hear him. The only possible excuse which can be offered for that captain's behavior is that his staggering was due not to the motion of the ship but to alcoholic stimulant. Could you imagine Little Sure Shot, the Terror of the Pawnees, drunk or sober, doing an asinine thing like that? Not in ten thousand years, you couldn't. But then we must remember that Little Sure Shot, being a moral dime-novel hero, never indulged in alcoholic beverages under any circumstances.

The boy who stood on the burning deck has been played up as an example of youthful heroism for the benefit of the young of our race ever since Mrs. Felicia Dorothea Hemans set him down in black and white. I deny that he was heroic. I insist that he merely was feeble-minded. Let us give this youth the careful once-over: The scene is the Battle of the Nile. The time is August, 1798. When the action of the piece begins the boy stands on the burning deck whence all but him had fled. You see, everyone else aboard had had sense enough to beat it, but he stuck because his father had posted him there. There was no good purpose he might serve by sticking, except to furnish added material for the poetess, but like the leather-headed young imbecile that he was he stood there with his feet getting warmer all the time, while the flame that lit the battle's wreck shone round him o'er the dead. After which:

There came a burst of thunder sound;
The boy—oh! where was he!
Ask of the winds, that far around
With fragments strewed the sea—

Ask the waves. Ask the fragments. Ask Mrs. Hemans. Or, to save time, inquire of me.

He has become totally extinct. He is no more and he never was very much. Still we need not worry. Mentally he must have been from the very outset a liability rather than an asset. Had he lived, undoubtedly he would have wound up in a home for the feeble-minded. It is better so, as it is—better that he should be spread about over the surface of the ocean in a broad general way, thus saving all the expense and trouble of gathering him up and burying him and putting a tombstone over him. He was one of the incurables.

Once upon a time, writing a little piece on another subject, I advanced the claim that the champion half-wit of all poetic anthology was Sweet Alice, who, as described by Mr. English, wept with delight when you gave her a smile, and trembled in fear at your frown. This of course was long before Prohibition came in. These times there are many ready to weep with delight when you offer to give them a smile; but in Mr. English's time and Alice's there were plenty of saloons handy. I remarked, what an awful kill-joy Alice must have been, weeping in a disconcerting manner when somebody smiled in her direction and trembling violently should anybody so much as merely knit his brow!

But when I gave Alice first place in the list I acted too hastily. Second thought should have informed me that undeniably the post of honor belonged to the central figure of Mr. Henry W. Longfellow's poem, Excelsior. I ran across it—Excelsior, I mean—in three different readers the other day when I was compiling some of the data for this treatise. Naturally it would be featured in all three. It wouldn't do to leave Mr. Longfellow's hero out of a volume in which space was given to such lesser village idiots as Casabianca and the Spartan youth. Let us take up this sad case verse by verse:

The shades of night were falling fast,
As through an Alpine village passed
A youth, who bore, 'mid snow and ice,
A banner with the strange device,
Excelsior!

There we get an accurate pen picture of this young man's deplorable state. He is climbing a mountain in the dead of winter. It is made plain later on that he is a stranger in the neighborhood, consequently it is fair to assume that the mountain in question is one he has never climbed before. Nobody hired him to climb any mountain; he isn't climbing it on a bet or because somebody dared him to climb one. He is not dressed for mountain climbing. Apparently he is wearing the costume in which he escaped from the institution where he had been an inmate—a costume consisting simply of low stockings, sandals and a kind of flowing woolen nightshirt, cut short to begin with and badly shrunken in the wash. He has on no rubber boots, no sweater, not even a pair of ear muffs. He also is bare-headed. Well, any time the wearing of hats went out of fashion he could have had no use for his head, anyhow.

I grant you that in the poem Mr. Longfellow does not go into details regarding the patient's garb. I am going by the illustration in the reader. The original Mr. McGuffey was very strong for illustrations. He stuck them in everywhere in his readers, whether they matched the themes or not. Being as fond of pictures as he undoubtedly was, it seems almost a pity he did not marry the tattooed lady in a circus and then when he got tired of studying her pictorially on one side he could ask her to turn around and let him see what she had to say on the other side. Perhaps he did. I never gleaned much regarding the family history of the McGuffeys.

Be that as it may, the wardrobe is entirely unsuited for the rigors of the climate in Switzerland in winter time. Symptomatically it marks the wearer as a person who is mentally lacking. He needs a keeper almost as badly as he needs some heavy underwear. But this isn't the worst of it. Take the banner. It bears the single word "Excelsior." The youth is going through a strange town late in the evening in his nightie, and it winter time, carrying a banner advertising a shredded wood-fiber commodity which won't be invented until a hundred and fifty years after he is dead!

Can you beat it? You can't even tie it.
Let us look further into the matter:

His brow was sad; his eyes beneath

Flashed like a falchion from its sheath,
And like a silver clarion rung
The accents of that unknown tongue,
Excelsior!

Get it, don't you? Even his features fail to jibe. His brow is corrugated with grief, but the flashing of the eye denotes a lack of intellectual coherence which any alienist would diagnose at a glance as evidence of total dementia, even were not confirmatory proof offered by his action in huckstering for a product which doesn't exist, in a language which no one present can understand. The most delirious typhoid fever patient you ever saw would know better than that.

To continue:

In happy homes he saw the light
Of household fires gleam warm and bright;
Above, the spectral glaciers shone,
And from his lips escaped a groan,
Excelsior!

The last line gives him away still more completely. He is groaning now, where a moment before he was clarioning. A bit later, with one of those shifts characteristic of the mentally unbalanced, his mood changes and again he is shouting. He's worse than a cuckoo clock, that boy.

"Try not the Pass," the old man said;
"Dark lowers the tempest overhead,

The roaring torrent is deep and wide!"
And loud that clarion voice replied,
Excelsior!

"Oh stay," the maiden said, "and rest

Thy weary head upon this breast!"
A tear stood in his bright blue eye,
But still he answered, with a sigh,
Excelsior!

"Beware the pine-tree's withered branch!
Beware the awful avalanche!"
This was the peasant's last Good night;
A voice replied, far up the height, Excelsior!

These three verses round out the picture. The venerable citizen warns him against the Pass; pass privileges up that mountain have all been suspended. A kind-hearted maiden tenders hospitalities of a most generous nature, considering that she never saw the young man before. Some people might even go so far as to say that she should have been ashamed of herself; others, that Mr. Longfellow, in giving her away, was guilty of an indelicacy, to say the least of it. Possibly she was practicing up to qualify for membership on the reception committee the next time the visiting firemen came to her town or when there was going to be an Elks' reunion; so I for one shall not question her motives. She was hospitable—let it go at that. The peasant couples with his good-night message a reference to the danger of falling pine wood and also avalanches, which have never been pleasant things to meet up with when one is traveling on a mountain in an opposite direction.

All about him firelights are gleaming, happy families are gathered before the hearthstone, and through the windows the evening yodel may be heard percolating pleasantly. There is every inducement for the youth to drop in and rest his poor, tired, foolish face and hands and thaw out his knee joints and give the maiden a chance to make good on that proposition of hers. But no, high up above timber line he has an engagement with himself and Mr. Longfellow to be frozen as stiff as a dried herring; and so, now groaning, now with his eye flashing, now with a tear—undoubtedly a frozen tear—standing in the eye, now clarioning, now sighing, onward and upward he goes:

At break of day, as heavenward
The pious monks of Saint Bernard
Uttered the oft-repeated prayer,
A voice cried through the startled air,
Excelsior!

I'll say this much for him: He certainly is hard to kill. He can stay out all night in those clothes, with the thermometer below zero, and at dawn still be able to chirp the only word that is left in his vocabulary. He can't last forever though. There has to be a finish to this lamentable fiasco sometime. We get it:

A traveler, by the faithful hound,
Half buried in the snow was found,
Still grasping in his hand of ice
That banner with the strange device,
Excelsior!

There in the twilight cold and gray,
Lifeless, but beautiful, he lay,
And from the sky serene and far,
A voice fell, like a falling star,
Excelsior!

The meteoric voice said "Excelsior !" It should have said "Bonehead!" It would have said it, too, if Ned Buntline had been handling the subject, for he had a sense of verities, had Ned. Probably that was one of the reasons why they barred his works out of all the schoolbooks.

With the passage of years I rather imagine that Lieutenant G—, of the United States Navy, who went to so much trouble and took so many needless pains in order to become a corpse may have vanished from the school readers. I admit I failed to find him in any of the modern editions through which I glanced, but I am able to report, as a result of my researches, that the well-known croupe specialist, Young Lochinvar, is still there, and so likewise is Casabianca, the total loss; and as I said before, I ran across Excelsior three times.

Just here the other day, when I was preparing the material for this little book, I happened upon an advertisement in a New York paper of an auction sale of a collection of so-called dime novels, dating back to the old Beadle's Boy's Library in the early eighties and coming on down through the years into the generation when Nick and Old Cap were succeeding some of the earlier favorites. I read off a few of the leading titles upon the list:

Bronze Jack, the California Thoroughbred; or, The Lost City of the Basaltic Buttes. A strange story of a desperate adventure after fortune in the weird, wild Apache land. By Albert W. Aiken.

Tombstone Dick, the Train Pilot; or, The Traitor's Trail. A story of the Arizona Wilds. By Ned Buntline.

The Tarantula of Taos; or, Giant George's Revenge. A tale of Sardine-box City, Arizona. By Major Sam S. (Buckskin Sam) Hall.

Redtop Rube, the Vigilante Prince; or, The Black Regulators of Arizona. By Major E. L. St. Vrain.

Old Grizzly Adams, the Bear Tamer; or, The Monarch of the Mountains.

Deadly Eye and the Prairie Rover.

Arizona Joe, the Boy Pard of Texas Jack.

Pacific Pete, the Prince of the Revolver.

Kit Carson, King of the Guides.

Leadville Nick, the Boy Sport; or, The Mad Miner's Revenge.

Lighthouse Lige; or, The Firebrand of the Everglades.

The Desperate Dozen; or, The Fair Fiend.

Nighthawk Kit; or, The Daughter of the Ranch.

Joaquin, the Saddle King.

Mustang Sam, the Wild Rider of the Plains.

Adventures of Wild Bill, the Pistol Prince, from Youth to his Death by Assassination. Deeds of Daring, Adventure and Thrilling Incidents in the Life of J. B. Hickok, known to the World as Wild Bill.

These titles and many another did I read, and reading them my mind slid back along a groove in my brain to a certain stable loft in a certain Kentucky town, and I said to myself that if I had a boy—say, about twelve or fourteen years old—I would go to this auction and bid in these books and I would back them up and re-enforce them with some of the best of the collected works of Nick Carter and Cap Collier and Nick Carter, Jr., and Frank Reade, and I would buy, if I could find it anywhere, a certain paper-backed volume dealing with the life of the James boys—not Henry and William, but Jesse and Frank—which I read ever so long ago; and. I would confer the whole lot of them upon that offspring of mine and I would say to him:

"Here, my son, is something for you; a rare and precious gift. Read these volumes openly. Never mind the crude style in which most of them are written. It can't be any worse than the stilted and artificial style in which your school reader is written; and, anyhow, if you are ever going to be a writer, style is a thing which you laboriously must learn, and then having acquired added wisdom you will forget part of it and chuck the rest of it out of the window and acquire a style of your own, which merely is another way of saying that if you have good taste to start with you will have what is called style in writing, and if you haven't that sense of good taste you won't have a style and nothing can give it to you.

"Read them for the thrills that are in them. Read them, remembering that if this country had not had a pioneer breed of Buckskin Sams and Deadwood Dicks we should have had no native school of which they, they in their turn, read when they were boys of your age.

"I refer, my son, to a book called Huckleberry Finn, and to a book called Treasure Island."

THE END

The Codes Of Hammurabi And Moses
W. W. Davies

QTY

The discovery of the Hammurabi Code is one of the greatest achievements of archaeology, and is of paramount interest, not only to the student of the Bible, but also to all those interested in ancient history...

Religion   **ISBN:** *1-59462-338-4*   **Pages:132**
MSRP $12.95

The Theory of Moral Sentiments
Adam Smith

QTY

This work from 1749. contains original theories of conscience amd moral judgment and it is the foundation for systemof morals.

Philosophy   **ISBN:** *1-59462-777-0*   **Pages:536**
MSRP $19.95

Jessica's First Prayer
Hesba Stretton

QTY

In a screened and secluded corner of one of the many railway-bridges which span the streets of London there could be seen a few years ago, from five o'clock every morning until half past eight, a tidily set-out coffee-stall, consisting of a trestle and board, upon which stood two large tin cans, with a small fire of charcoal burning under each so as to keep the coffee boiling during the early hours of the morning when the work-people were thronging into the city on their way to their daily toil...

Pages:84

Childrens   **ISBN:** *1-59462-373-2*   *MSRP $9.95*

My Life and Work
Henry Ford

QTY

Henry Ford revolutionized the world with his implementation of mass production for the Model T automobile. Gain valuable business insight into his life and work with his own auto-biography... "We have only started on our development of our country we have not as yet, with all our talk of wonderful progress, done more than scratch the surface. The progress has been wonderful enough but..."

Pages:300

Biographies/   **ISBN:** *1-59462-198-5*   *MSRP $21.95*

The Art of Cross-Examination
Francis Wellman

QTY

I presume it is the experience of every author, after his first book is published upon an important subject, to be almost overwhelmed with a wealth of ideas and illustrations which could readily have been included in his book, and which to his own mind, at least, seem to make a second edition inevitable. Such certainly was the case with me; and when the first edition had reached its sixth impression in five months, I rejoiced to learn that it seemed to my publishers that the book had met with a sufficiently favorable reception to justify a second and considerably enlarged edition. ..

Pages:412

Reference   ISBN: *1-59462-647-2*   *MSRP $19.95*

On the Duty of Civil Disobedience
Henry David Thoreau

QTY

Thoreau wrote his famous essay, On the Duty of Civil Disobedience, as a protest against an unjust but popular war and the immoral but popular institution of slave-owning. He did more than write—he declined to pay his taxes,   and was hauled off to gaol in consequence. Who can say how much this refusal of his hastened the end of the war and of slavery ?

Law   ISBN: *1-59462-747-9*   **Pages:48**

MSRP $7.45

Dream Psychology Psychoanalysis for Beginners
Sigmund Freud

QTY

Sigmund Freud, born Sigismund Schlomo Freud (May 6, 1856 - September 23, 1939), was a Jewish-Austrian neurologist and psychiatrist who co-founded the psychoanalytic school of psychology. Freud is best known for his theories of the unconscious mind, especially involving the mechanism of repression; his redefinition of sexual desire as mobile and directed towards a wide variety of objects; and his therapeutic techniques, especially his understanding of transference in the therapeutic relationship and the presumed value of dreams as sources of insight into unconscious desires.

Pages:196

Psychology   ISBN: *1-59462-905-6*   *MSRP $15.45*

The Miracle of Right Thought
Orison Swett Marden

QTY

Believe with all of your heart that you will do what you were made to do. When the mind has once formed the habit of holding cheerful, happy, prosperous pictures, it will not be easy to form the opposite habit. It does not matter how improbable or how far away this realization may see, or how dark the prospects may be, if we visualize them as best we can, as vividly as possible, hold tenaciously to them and vigorously struggle to attain them, they will gradually become actualized, realized in the life. But a desire, a longing without endeavor, a yearning abandoned or held indifferently will vanish without realization.

Pages:360

Self Help   ISBN: *1-59462-644-8*   *MSRP $25.45*

www.bookjungle.com *email: sales@bookjungle.com fax: 630-214-0564 mail: Book Jungle PO Box 2226 Champaign, IL 61825*

QTY

The Rosicrucian Cosmo-Conception Mystic Christianity *by Max Heindel*   ISBN: *1-59462-188-8*   **$38.95**
The Rosicrucian Cosmo-conception is not dogmatic, neither does it appeal to any other authority than the reason of the student. It is: not controversial, but is: sent forth in the, hope that it may help to clear...   *New Age/Religion Pages 646*

Abandonment To Divine Providence *by Jean-Pierre de Caussade*   ISBN: *1-59462-228-0*   **$25.95**
"The Rev. Jean Pierre de Caussade was one of the most remarkable spiritual writers of the Society of Jesus in France in the 18th Century. His death took place at Toulouse in 1751. His works have gone through many editions and have been republished...   *Inspirational/Religion Pages 400*

Mental Chemistry *by Charles Haanel*   ISBN: *1-59462-192-6*   **$23.95**
Mental Chemistry allows the change of material conditions by combining and appropriately utilizing the power of the mind. Much like applied chemistry creates something new and unique out of careful combinations of chemicals the mastery of mental chemistry...   *New Age Pages 354*

The Letters of Robert Browning and Elizabeth Barret Barrett 1845-1846 vol II   ISBN: *1-59462-193-4*   **$35.95**
by Robert Browning and Elizabeth Barrett   *Biographies Pages 596*

Gleanings In Genesis (volume I) *by Arthur W. Pink*   ISBN: *1-59462-130-6*   **$27.45**
Appropriately has Genesis been termed "the seed plot of the Bible" for in it we have, in germ form, almost all of the great doctrines which are afterwards fully developed in the books of Scripture which follow...   *Religion/Inspirational Pages 420*

The Master Key *by L. W. de Laurence*   ISBN: *1-59462-001-6*   **$30.95**
In no branch of human knowledge has there been a more lively increase of the spirit of research during the past few years than in the study of Psychology, Concentration and Mental Discipline. The requests for authentic lessons in Thought Control, Mental Discipline and...   *New Age/Business Pages 422*

The Lesser Key Of Solomon Goetia *by L. W. de Laurence*   ISBN: *1-59462-092-X*   **$9.95**
This translation of the first book of the "Lernegton" which is now for the first time made accessible to students of Talismanic Magic was done, after careful collation and edition, from numerous Ancient Manuscripts in Hebrew, Latin, and French...   *New Age/Occult Pages 92*

Rubaiyat Of Omar Khayyam *by Edward Fitzgerald*   ISBN:*1-59462-332-5*   **$13.95**
Edward Fitzgerald, whom the world has already learned, in spite of his own efforts to remain within the shadow of anonymity, to look upon as one of the rarest poets of the century, was born at Bredfield, in Suffolk, on the 31st of March, 1809. He was the third son of John Purcell...   *Music Pages 172*

Ancient Law *by Henry Maine*   ISBN: *1-59462-128-4*   **$29.95**
The chief object of the following pages is to indicate some of the earliest ideas of mankind, as they are reflected in Ancient Law, and to point out the relation of those ideas to modern thought.   *Religiom/History Pages 452*

Far-Away Stories *by William J. Locke*   ISBN: *1-59462-129-2*   **$19.45**
"Good wine needs no bush, but a collection of mixed vintages does. And this book is just such a collection. Some of the stories I do not want to remain buried for ever in the museum files of dead magazine-numbers an author's not unpardonable vanity..."   *Fiction Pages 272*

Life of David Crockett *by David Crockett*   ISBN: *1-59462-250-7*   **$27.45**
"Colonel David Crockett was one of the most remarkable men of the times in which he lived. Born in humble life, but gifted with a strong will, an indomitable courage, and unremitting perseverance...   *Biographies/New Age Pages 424*

Lip-Reading *by Edward Nitchie*   ISBN: *1-59462-206-X*   **$25.95**
Edward B. Nitchie, founder of the New York School for the Hard of Hearing, now the Nitchie School of Lip-Reading, Inc, wrote "LIP-READING Principles and Practice". The development and perfecting of this meritorious work on lip-reading was an undertaking...   *How-to Pages 400*

A Handbook of Suggestive Therapeutics, Applied Hypnotism, Psychic Science   ISBN: *1-59462-214-0*   **$24.95**
by Henry Munro   *Health/New Age/Health/Self-help Pages 376*

A Doll's House: and Two Other Plays *by Henrik Ibsen*   ISBN: *1-59462-112-8*   **$19.95**
Henrik Ibsen created this classic when in revolutionary 1848 Rome. Introducing some striking concepts in playwriting for the realist genre, this play has been studied the world over.   *Fiction/Classics/Plays 308*

The Light of Asia *by sir Edwin Arnold*   ISBN: *1-59462-204-3*   **$13.95**
In this poetic masterpiece, Edwin Arnold describes the life and teachings of Buddha. The man who was to become known as Buddha to the world was born as Prince Gautama of India but he rejected the worldly riches and abandoned the reigns of power when...   *Religion/History/Biographies Pages 170*

The Complete Works of Guy de Maupassant *by Guy de Maupassant*   ISBN: *1-59462-157-8*   **$16.95**
"For days and days, nights and nights, I had dreamed of that first kiss which was to consecrate our engagement, and I knew not on what spot I should put my lips..."   *Fiction/Classics Pages 240*

The Art of Cross-Examination *by Francis L. Wellman*   ISBN: *1-59462-309-0*   **$26.95**
Written by a renowned trial lawyer, Wellman imparts his experience and uses case studies to explain how to use psychology to extract desired information through questioning.   *How-to/Science/Reference Pages 408*

Answered or Unanswered? *by Louisa Vaughan*   ISBN: *1-59462-248-5*   **$10.95**
Miracles of Faith in China   *Religion Pages 112*

The Edinburgh Lectures on Mental Science (1909) *by Thomas*   ISBN: *1-59462-008-3*   **$11.95**
This book contains the substance of a course of lectures recently given by the writer in the Queen Street Hail, Edinburgh. Its purpose is to indicate the Natural Principles governing the relation between Mental Action and Material Conditions...   *New Age Psychology Pages 148*

Ayesha *by H. Rider Haggard*   ISBN: *1-59462-301-5*   **$24.95**
Verily and indeed it is the unexpected that happens! Probably if there was one person upon the earth from whom the Editor of this, and of a certain previous history, did not expect to hear again...   *Classics Pages 380*

Ayala's Angel *by Anthony Trollope*   ISBN: *1-59462-352-X*   **$29.95**
The two girls were both pretty, but Lucy who was twenty-one who supposed to be simple and comparatively unattractive, whereas Ayala was credited, as her Bombwhat romantic name might show, with poetic charm and a taste for romance. Ayala when her father died was nineteen...   *Fiction Pages 484*

The American Commonwealth *by James Bryce*   ISBN: *1-59462-286-8*   **$34.45**
An interpretation of American democratic political theory. It examines political mechanics and society from the perspective of Scotsman James Bryce   *Politics Pages 572*

Stories of the Pilgrims *by Margaret P. Pumphrey*   ISBN: *1-59462-116-0*   **$17.95**
This book explores pilgrims religious oppression in England as well as their escape to Holland and eventual crossing to America on the Mayflower, and their early days in New England...   *History Pages 268*

QTY

The Fasting Cure by *Sinclair Upton*   ISBN: *1-59462-222-1* **$13.95**
In the Cosmopolitan Magazine for May, 1910, and in the Contemporary Review (London) for April, 1910, I published an article dealing with my experiences in fasting. I have written a great many magazine articles, but never one which attracted so much attention... New Age/Self Help/Health Pages 164

Hebrew Astrology by *Sepharial*   ISBN: *1-59462-308-2* **$13.45**
In these days of advanced thinking it is a matter of common observation that we have left many of the old landmarks behind and that we are now pressing forward to greater heights and to a wider horizon than that which represented the mind-content of our progenitors... Astrology Pages 144

Thought Vibration or The Law of Attraction in the Thought World   ISBN: *1-59462-127-6* **$12.95**

by *William Walker Atkinson*   *Psychology/Religion Pages 144*

Optimism by *Helen Keller*   ISBN: *1-59462-108-X* **$15.95**
Helen Keller was blind, deaf, and mute since 19 months old, yet famously learned how to overcome these handicaps, communicate with the world, and spread her lectures promoting optimism. An inspiring read for everyone... Biographies/Inspirational Pages 84

Sara Crewe by *Frances Burnett*   ISBN: *1-59462-360-0* **$9.45**
In the first place, Miss Minchin lived in London. Her home was a large, dull, tall one, in a large, dull square, where all the houses were alike, and all the sparrows were alike, and where all the door-knockers made the same heavy sound... Childrens/Classic Pages 88

The Autobiography of Benjamin Franklin by *Benjamin Franklin*   ISBN: *1-59462-135-7* **$24.95**
The Autobiography of Benjamin Franklin has probably been more extensively read than any other American historical work, and no other book of its kind has had such ups and downs of fortune. Franklin lived for many years in England, where he was agent... Biographies/History Pages 332

Name	
Email	
Telephone	
Address	
City, State ZIP	

☐ Credit Card   ☐ Check / Money Order

Credit Card Number	
Expiration Date	
Signature	

Please Mail to: Book Jungle
                            PO Box 2226
                            Champaign, IL 61825
or Fax to: 630-214-0564